CLOUDY with a chance of MEAT BALLS™

The Weather Report
WITH SAM SPARKS

by Alison Inches
illustrated by Brigette Barrager

Simon Spotlight
New York London Toronto Sydney

SIMON SPOTLIGHT
An imprint of Simon & Schuster
Children's Publishing Division
1230 Avenue of the Americas,
New York, New York 10020

Manufactured in the United States of America
First Edition 10 9 8 7 6 5 4 3 2 1
ISBN 978-1-4169-6734-7

Read the original book by
Judi Barrett and Ron Barrett

Hello, America! I'm Sam Sparks reporting live for the Weather News Network. Hungry for a juicy weather report? Well, get ready. You're not going to believe it, but it's raining cheeseburgers in the small town of Swallow Falls! Just look at all those plump, juicy cheeseburgers falling down from the sky. This is the best tasting weather, well, ever!

Good morning, everybody in Swallow Falls! It's time to tuck in your napkins and get your sunny-sides up. As you can see, a breakfast system is just moving into the area, and you're going to flip for my forecast. It looks like we're going to have pancake showers mixed with fried eggs, bacon, and orange juice! By lunchtime the clouds will shift and we'll have steady pizza rains with extra cheese. It'll be partly sunny in the afternoon with a hot-dog storm heading in for dinner.

Be sure to carry an umbrella and wear a light rain jacket to avoid food stains. Also make sure you drive carefully around lunchtime. The streets will be slick with melted mozzarella!

DON'T TALK WITH YOUR MOUTH FULL

MEN AT LUNCH

Hi, everyone! Sam Sparks for the Weather News Network here with your up-to-the-minute weather report. Well, the heavens have let loose, and the weather keeps getting tastier! I've just come from an exclusive interview with famous inventor Flint Lockwood, and I've got the scoop on your five-day dessert forecast:

MONDAY	TUESDAY	WEDNESDAY
CHOCOLATE-CHIP COOKIES	CUPCAKES	JELLY BEANS
62°	70°	60°

Hey, Sam Sparks here! Today's top weather story—and the one thing on every viewer's mind—what does this town do with all the *leftovers*? Well, what the mayor doesn't eat gets tossed into the Outtasighter. Flint Lockwood's latest invention catapults uneaten food out of sight *and* out of mind.

SARDINE WASTE MANAGEMENT

Do I have a weather scoop for you: It's snowing ice cream! There must be at least thirty-one flavors on the ground. And here's the cherry on top—the mayor has declared today a snow day in Chewandswallow! That's right, school's out! So kids, put your snow gear on and grab a spoon. Parents, make sure you keep an eye on them. It's pretty slippery out here!

On a serious note ice-cream accumulations will be heavy today and continue on into this evening. Stay off the roads if possible! As the temperature warms up this afternoon those ice-cream scoops will quickly melt into ice-cream soup, but as it cools down again this evening that colorful, slippery coating will leave a dangerous mark.

Hello, everyone! Today's weather looks super–*supersized*–that is. Everyone here loves the new, larger portions . . . but it almost seems like it might be too much. However, even though enormous steaks are pounding the community, there are some meat lovers that don't seem to mind.

Seriously, you guys, these portions are beginning to pose a threat to this town. Giant hot dogs are crashing into homes and injuring people.

Mr. Mayor, do you have anything to say about all this?

"I say, bigger is better—right? Come visit our Nacho Cheese Hot Springs. Climb Mount Leftovers! Bring the family and enjoy!"

Well, I guess there you have it. Still, I urge people to stay inside if you can. It's getting dangerous out here.

Alert! Citizens of Chewandswallow, I'm Sam Sparks, and this is an emergency broadcast! A spaghetti-and-meatball twister is roaring through town. Head to your basement! Get to a shelter! The food machine is out of control! I repeat: Giant meatballs are headed our way, and everyone needs to take cover!

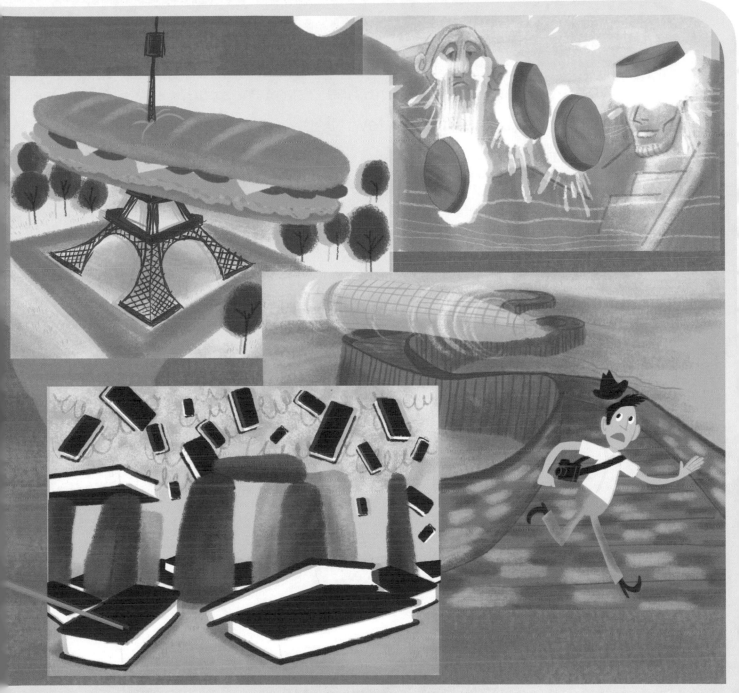

People of Chewandswallow, things have gotten serious. I urge you to stay in your homes. If your home has been smashed, crushed, or damaged, jump on a bread boat down by the dock. They are taking citizens away to safety.

BEWARE OF GIANT DOUGHNUTS

And now this special announcement: We're going to go inside the food weather machine to try and shut it down. We won't be able to televise this mission as we are headed inside the food asteroid. Hopefully we will have some good news for you soon.

Please stay tuned!

Several hours later . . .

Ka-BOOOM!

Sam Sparks here, and we've just landed. As you can see from the huge explosion the shutdown mission has been a success. However I'm so sad to report that during the mission we may have lost our town's hero, Flint. He was a great man. Although, wait, what is that up above?

Faithful viewers around the world, we have good news to report: Flint Lockwood has been rescued by one of his very own inventions— Ratbirds! I can't believe it! And look, the clouds are clearing! It looks like this afternoon's forecast will include sunny skies!

I'm so thrilled to be reporting such a happy ending. Make sure you tune in daily for more exciting news and weather stories. For the Weather News Network, I'm Sam Sparks!

WEATHER NEWS NETWORK